Who Grew My SOUP?

Written by Tom Darbyshire
Illustrated by C. F. Payne

This book was underwritten by the Campbell Soup Company,
in hopes that children of all ages will learn to love to eat their vegetables.

© 2012 Publications International, Ltd.
Text and illustrations © 2010 Campbell Soup Company

Published by Louis Weber, C.E.O., Publications International, Ltd.
7373 North Cicero Avenue, Lincolnwood, Illinois 60712
Ground Floor, 59 Gloucester Place, London W1U 8JJ

Customer Service: 1-800-595-8484 or customer_service@pilbooks.com

www.pilcookbooks.com

p i kids is a trademark of Publications International, Ltd.,
and is registered in the United States.

8 7 6 5 4 3 2 1

Manufactured in USA.

ISBN-13: 978-1-4508-6645-3
ISBN-10: 1-4508-6645-X

Lesson Plan & Extension Activities

Lesson Procedure:

1. Introduce the My New York Plate poster, preferably post it on the white-board. Explain each of the five food groups one at a time, introducing the story of the farmer in each category.

2. Have the students brainstorm any products they know that fit in each of the categories. Write their answers next to the corresponding section of the poster on the board. Help them fill in any they may not know.

3. When all five food groups have been reviewed and the food lists created, ask the students how each of them makes their bodies healthy.

4. Go over the food lists and circle or star all of the foods grown or produced in New York. Tell the students that the farmers in our state grow hundreds of different types of crops such as the ones they have just identified.

Activity Procedure:

1. Tell students that each day they should eat from the five food groups for a healthy diet - review that they are vegetables, fruits, grains, protein, and dairy. Have them hold up one hand and list the five food groups, one for each finger. After they list the five food groups, have them turn to a partner and give each other a high five.

2. Each student will need a pre-cut paper hand, a tongue depressor, tape, and crayons.

3. On one side of the hand students write the name of a food group on each finger. In the center of the palm they write "Exercise Daily." On the other side of the hand the students should write/draw a New York grown food for each food group in the corresponding finger area. They will write/draw their favorite exercise in the palm area.

4. Tape a tongue depressor at the wrist area.

Program Conclusion:

- Present the book to the teacher and students as a donation to the classroom or school library.
- Ask the students as a group to repeat the five food groups. Have the students take turns sharing their favorite New York foods with the class.

Five Food Groups & Key Messages

Fruits and Vegetables: Any fruit or vegetable is included in this group. Fruits or vegetables may be fresh, canned , frozen, or dried.

Key Message: Make half your plate fruits and vegetables.

Grains: Any food made from wheat, rice, oats, cornmeal, barley, or another cereal grain is a grain product. Examples include bread, pasta, oatmeal, breakfast cereals, tortillas, and grits.

Key Message: Make at least half of your grains whole grains.

Protein: All foods made from meat, poultry, seafood, beans and peas, eggs, processed soy products, nuts and seeds are considered part of this group.

Key Message: Choose lean protein.

Dairy: All fluid milk products and many foods made from milk are considered part of this food group. Foods made from milk that retain their calcium content are part of the group, such as cheese and yogurt.

Key Message: Choose fat-free or low-fat dairy products.

For more information, visit: http://www.choosemyplate.gov/food-groups/

Are you looking for more lessons on nutrition and farmers related to *Who Grew My Soup?*

New York Agriculture in the Classroom has a section of the website dedicated to additional lesson plans, vocabulary games, and activities for learning extensions on this included lesson. Find more information at:

http://www.agclassroom.org/ny/programs/literacy.htm

Variety of commodities produced in New York State

New York is a highly productive state in the variety and amount of agricultural commodities that are produced. To learn more about the many types of agricultural products, and the economic impact of ag in New York, visit:

http://www.agriculture.ny.gov/agfacts.html

Teacher Program Evaluation

Win an Agriculture in the Classroom prize pack just for teachers! Please take a few short moments to follow the link below and complete a survey to evaluate the Agricultural Literacy Week program, resources, and the presentation that took place in your classroom.

Teacher feedback is invaluable, and helps to shape the direction of all of our programs.

Follow the web address below and complete this evaluation before May 1, 2014. Multiple teacher names will be drawn at random to win prize packs of a $50 value.

https://www.surveymonkey.com/s/ALW2014Teachers

Non-Fiction Farmer Stories

To read more about the farmer's featured on the *My New York Plate* poster, see pictures from their farm, and learn more about their farm's stories please visit the link below.

If you know of a farmer who would like to share their farm story with student's across the state, please put them in contact with New York Agriculture in the Classroom.

http://www.agclassroom.org/ny/programs/literacy.htm

Vocabulary

Nutritious—Having substances that a person or animal needs to be healthy and grow properly; promoting good health and growth.

Suspicious—causing or showing a feeling that something is wrong or that someone is behaving wrongly.

Vegetable—The edible part of a plant.

Chemical Additives—Substances added to food to preserve flavor or enhance its taste and appearance.

Processed Food—Commercially prepared food designed for ease of consumption.

Summon—To order someone to come to a place. To send or call for someone or something.

Green Thumb—An unusual ability to make plants grow.

Vegetables Mentioned in the Book

Carrot—The long orange edible root of a common garden plant that is eaten as a vegetable.

Tomato—A round, soft, red fruit that is eaten raw or cooked and that is often used in salads, sandwiches, sauces, etc.

Beans—A seed that is eaten as a vegetable and that comes from many different kinds of climbing plants. A part of a plant that contains very young seeds.

Barley—A cereal grass; its seed is used especially in foods (as soups and cereals), or as livestock feed.

Corn—The seeds of a cereal plant.

Potato—A round root of a plant; a thick starchy edible underground tubers.

Spinach—A plant with dark green leaves.

Peas—Part of the legume family; grown for its pods of protein rich edible rounded seeds.

Celery—Related to the carrot; has thick edible stems.

Additional Information and Resources

<u>Books:</u>

To Market, To Market
by Nikki McClure
This book follows a mother and a son to a weekly farmer's market. As they check items off their shopping list, the reader learns how each food was grown or produced.

How Did That Get in my Lunchbox? The Story of Food
by Chris Butterworth
How did that delicious food get in your lunchbox? This is a clear, engaging look at the steps involved in producing some common foods.

<u>Websites:</u>

Fresh From the World: Where Your Food Comes From
http://urbanext.illinois.edu/food/

Mapmaker Interactive—National Geographic Education
http://education.nationalgeographic.com/education/mapping/interactive-map/?ar_a=1

<u>Videos:</u>

I'm Farming and I Grow It
http://www.youtube.com/watch?v=48H7zOQrX3U&feature=share&list=PLpniJUeAKfupMAobWOtCvEmjosZiPX07S&index=1

About New York Agriculture in the Classroom

Mission: To foster an awareness, understanding, and appreciation of how we produce food, fiber, natural resources by engaging educators and students with agriculture and food systems.

Department of Horticulture
Cornell University
Ithaca, NY 14853
607-255-9253
nyaitc@cornell.edu
agclassroom.org/ny

Agricultural Literacy Week
New York Agriculture in the Classroom
2014 Educator Resource Guide

Dear Educator,

Thank you for welcoming agricultural literacy volunteers into your classroom. One of the best ways to celebrate National Agriculture Week is to participate in Agricultural Literacy Week, joining thousands of teachers and tens of thousands of students in exploring the beauty and bounty of New York's food and fiber systems.

The question being asked throughout New York state school's this week is, *Who Grew My Soup?* This important question will be answered as volunteers read the story of Phineas Quinn to your students, and hopefully it will spark the inquiry in their minds to explore and meet the agricultural producers who grew their favorite foods. Nutrition begins on the farm, and strong connections with your farmers helps to inspire healthy lifestyle choices.

One out of every five students in your classroom will enter into an agricultural related field, with 20 percent of the American workforce engaged in a form of agriculture. New York Agriculture in the Classroom strives to create the next generation of agriculturally literate students and informed consumers, and we do that through assisting teachers in implementing agricultural concepts into their curriculum.

We would like to thank our teachers who find the time and opportunities for our volunteers to come into their classrooms, the more than 1,000 volunteers who read to more than 45,000 students, and the county Coordinators who make the event possible.

Sincerely,

Katie Bigness
Coordinator, New York Agriculture in the Classroom

Spring 2014 Agriculture in the Classroom Opportunities

- Earn up to 6 hours of professional development credit by participating in a *Food, Land and People* educator training at various locations across the state. The *Food, Land and People* curriculum is aligned to NYS and the Common Core Learning Standards, and includes 55 lessons developed and tested by thousands of educators.

- Involve your class in the *I Love NY Agriculture Art and Writing Contest*. Entries are due April 25, 2014. Entry forms are available on the website: www.agclassroom.org/ny

- The National Agriculture in the Classroom Conference will be in Hershey, PA from June 23 to June 27, 2014. Meet peer teachers from across the country and engage in professional development in increasing agricultural literacy in your curriculum. Learn more at: http://www.agclassroom.org/conference2014/index.htm

 Facebook.com/NYAITC   @NewYorkAITC   Pinterest.com/NYAITC

Mark Your Calendar

Next year's Agricultural Literacy Week will be held March 16-20, 2015. Join us again for great volunteers, and strong connections to our food and fiber systems in your classroom.

Who Grew My Soup? Lesson Plan

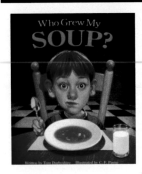

Grade Level: K-3

Common Core ELA Standards Met:

R.K.2, R.K.7, W.K.5, SL.K.1, SL.K.2, SL.K.5

R.1.1, R.1.2, R.1.4, SL.1.1, SL.1.2, SL.1.5

R.2.1, R.2.3, SL.2.1.b, SL.2.4

R.3.3, R.3.4, SL.3.1, SL.3.2, SL.3.4

Time: 30 minutes

Materials: *Who Grew My Soup?* book, the My New York Plate poster (or a MyPlate graphic), pre-cut handprint outline, tape, one tongue depressor per student, crayons

Extensions: For related lessons and extensions, please visit *http://www.agclassroom.org/ny/programs/literacy.htm*

Give Me Five

Adapted from Oregon Agriculture in the Classroom

Helpful Hints and Program Preparation:

- Make copies of the included hand print - one per student, and **pre-cut** the hands to ensure there is enough time to read the book and lead the activity. Students could not cut the hand, or cut around the fingers.

- Read the book and the activity plan several times before you work with your classes.

- You may want to use sticky notes on the pages of the book where you have specific talking points, or where you would like to ask the students questions.

Introduction (5 minutes):

1. Gather students together in the reading area of the classroom.

2. Introduce yourself and explain your relationship to agriculture and why agriculture is important to you.

3. Ask the students if they know a farmer in their family or in the community. If students do know farmers, ask them if they know what that farmer produces. If they do not know a farmer, ask them what they think farmers grow or produce in their community.

4. Explain the plan for your time together; you will be learning that good nutrition begins on the farm, about give New York farmers who produce food in the MyPlate categories, and identifying our favorite New York agriculture products.

Reading Aloud (10 minutes):

Read *Who Grew My Soup?* by Tom Darbyshire to the class. During the reading asking them such questions as:

- Why do you think Phineas Quinn did not want to try the soup?

- Have you ever tried a fresh carrot or tomato? What did it taste like? Why do you think Phineas liked his carrot and tomato so much?

Lesson and Activity (15 minutes):

Background:

Healthy food and good nutrition begins on a farm. Farmers are our neighbors, our friends, and local business owners whose products can be marketed and sold locally, nationally, or internationally. It's important to understand the variety of products grown in our community and state, and how those foods help to fuel our bodies by meeting the needs of the five food groups.

Objectives:

1. Identify the five major food groups.

2. Name at least three New York grown products in each food group.

3. Identify and draw one favorite New York food in each food group, and one favorite form of physical activity.

A boy of age ten, named Phineas Quinn,
   was out playing ball when his mom called him in.
"It's lunchtime," she said. "Here's something nutritious!"
   This instantly made young Phin Quinn most suspicious.
"It's yummy," she said, with a smile brightly beaming,
   as she gave him a bowl of soup, gently steaming.

Phin looked down and thought, **"YUCK!**
    It's vegetable **GUNK!**
The foods I prefer are the foods she calls **JUNK.**
    Fake colors and flavors?
Delicious and dandy!
    They're in all my favorite sodas and candy.
Chemical additives? **YUM!** They're the best!
    The snack foods I crave are preserved and processed.
I like stuff that's deep-fried, and loaded with sugars;
    but vegetable soup? Yikes! I'd rather eat **BOOGERS.**
This looks too healthy, I bet it tastes **ICKY…"**
    So Phin hatched a plan, and oh boy, was it tricky!

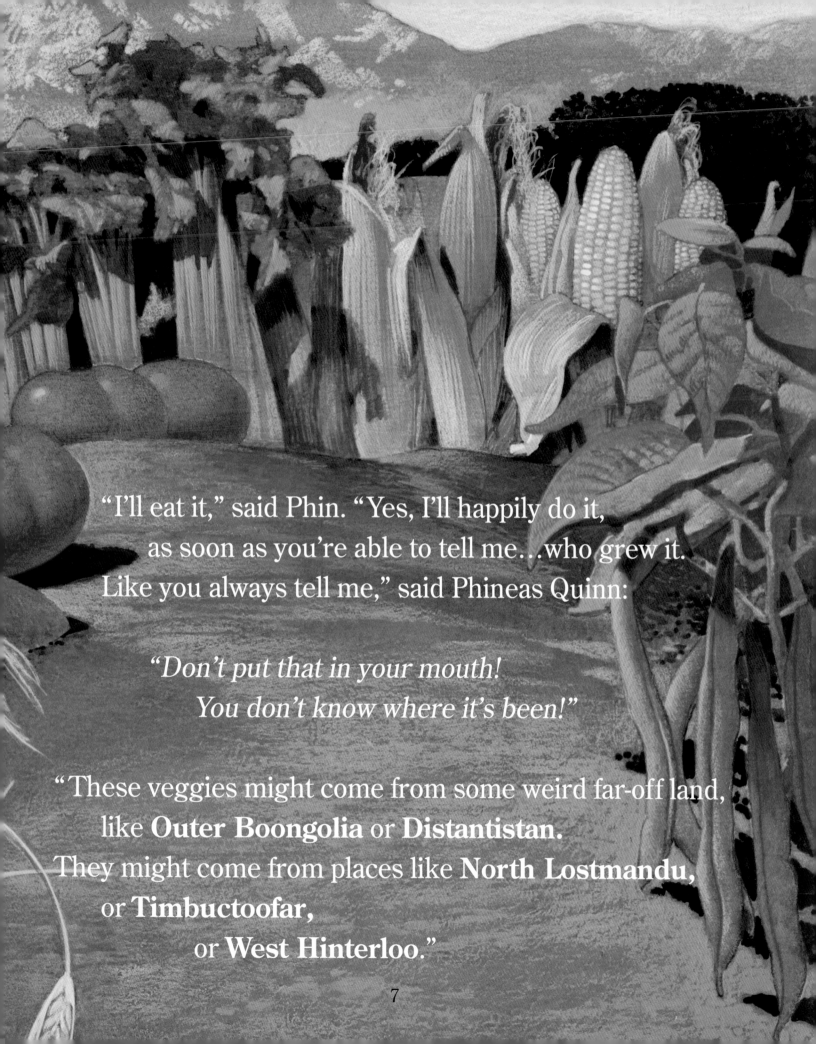

"I'll eat it," said Phin. "Yes, I'll happily do it,
    as soon as you're able to tell me…who grew it.
Like you always tell me," said Phineas Quinn:

"*Don't put that in your mouth!*
    You don't know where it's been!"

"These veggies might come from some weird far-off land,
    like **Outer Boongolia** or **Distantistan.**
They might come from places like **North Lostmandu,**
    or **Timbuctoofar,**
        or **West Hinterloo.**"

7

"Who grew these carrots?
Who grew these tomatoes?

These beans and this barley?
This corn? These potatoes?

Who sprouted this spinach?
Who planted these peas?

And who picked this celery?
Tell me now, please.

I'll not take one sip of this vegetable goop
unless you tell me this:

WHO GREW MY SOUP?"

While Phin thought himself oh-so-terribly clever,
he'd never have guessed what came next,
never-**EVER!**

His eyes popped,
    his jaw dropped,
        he fumbled his spoon.
From the sky came a flying tomato balloon!

The pilot, in goggles, was shouting hello,
    from a rather large cooking pot hanging below.
"Hop in!
    Hurry up!
        Climb aboard!
            Tallyho!"

"Where are we going?" Phin asked, most alarmed.
    "We're going," the man said, "to where soup is farmed!
I'm Mr. Mattoo, chief soup *soup*ervisor,
    and we won't come back until you're *souper*-wiser.

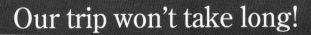

Our trip won't take long!
Not at all!
No indeed!
This balloon can achieve
*soup*ersonical speed."

As soon as he said it,
they flew away, **ZOOM!**
With a **WHOOSH!**
And a **WHIR!**
And a big sonic

BOOM!

Phin summoned his courage, he took a look down,
and found they were already back on the ground.

"Phin, meet Farmer Hitchner. Hitchner, meet Phin.
Mr. Hitchner's the farmer whose field we are in.
These carrots, this field, and this farm are all his.
Hitchner's a genius, a soup-growing whiz!"

"What carrots?" asked Phin as he looked all around.
"They're down here," said Hitchner,
"they grow underground."

"They grow in the **DIRT?**" Young Phin nearly gagged.
"Gee, I've only seen them in stores, washed and bagged."

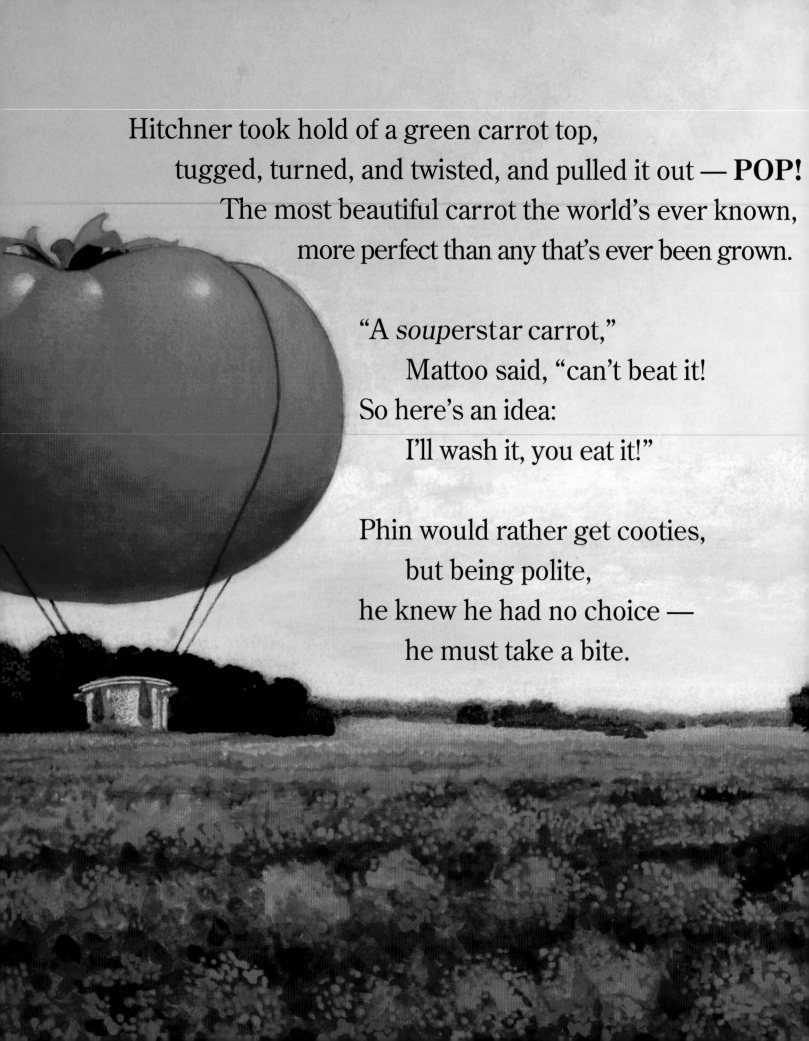

Hitchner took hold of a green carrot top,
tugged, turned, and twisted, and pulled it out — **POP!**
The most beautiful carrot the world's ever known,
more perfect than any that's ever been grown.

"A *soup*erstar carrot,"
    Mattoo said, "can't beat it!
So here's an idea:
    I'll wash it, you eat it!"

Phin would rather get cooties,
    but being polite,
he knew he had no choice —
    he must take a bite.

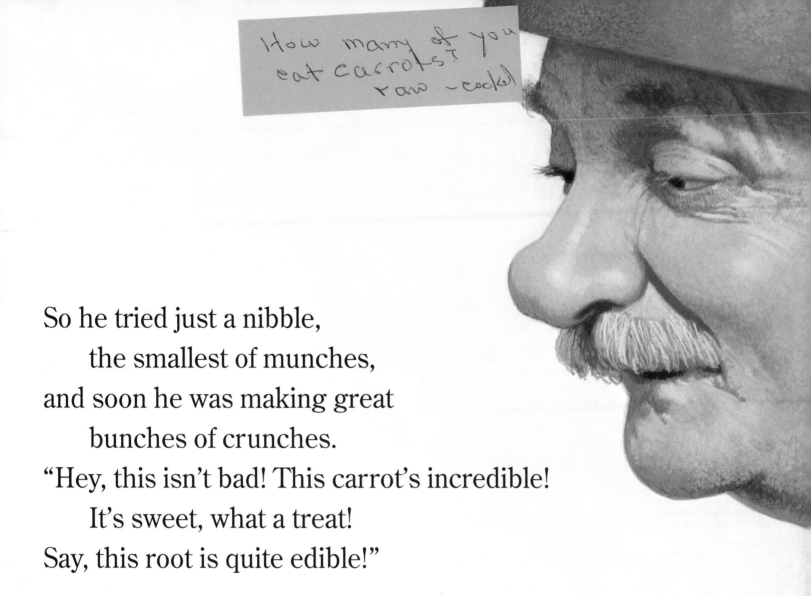

So he tried just a nibble,
    the smallest of munches,
and soon he was making great
    bunches of crunches.
"Hey, this isn't bad! This carrot's incredible!
    It's sweet, what a treat!
Say, this root is quite edible!"

"There's something in carrots," said Mr. Mattoo,
    "that is good for your eyesight. Amazing and true!
I eat them quite often. My vision is great.
    I can see at this moment that we're running late.
So toodle-oo, Hitchner! Come on, Phin, let's go!
    We've more places to see where more soup-veggies grow."

It seemed that no sooner than they'd left the ground,
they'd crossed seventeen states
and were dropping back down
in a field of tomatoes all ripe, red, and round.

"Phin, meet Farmer Perez, his thumbs are quite green,
the tomatoes he grows are the best ever seen!"

"Mmm, this is delicious!" nodded young Phin,
as red, ripe tomato juice ran down his chin.

"Oh good! *Souper*-duper!" cried Mr. Mattoo,
"*Souper*lative!
Come on!
We've lots more to do!"

Farm to farm,
　　field to field,
　　　　whiz! whiz! whiz!
　　　　　　through the sky.

From onions so fine they could make a man cry,
　　to potatoes,
　　　　to peas,
　　　　　　in the blink of an eye.

They stalked the best celery,
　　they got to know beans,
and met growers who know how to grow greener greens.

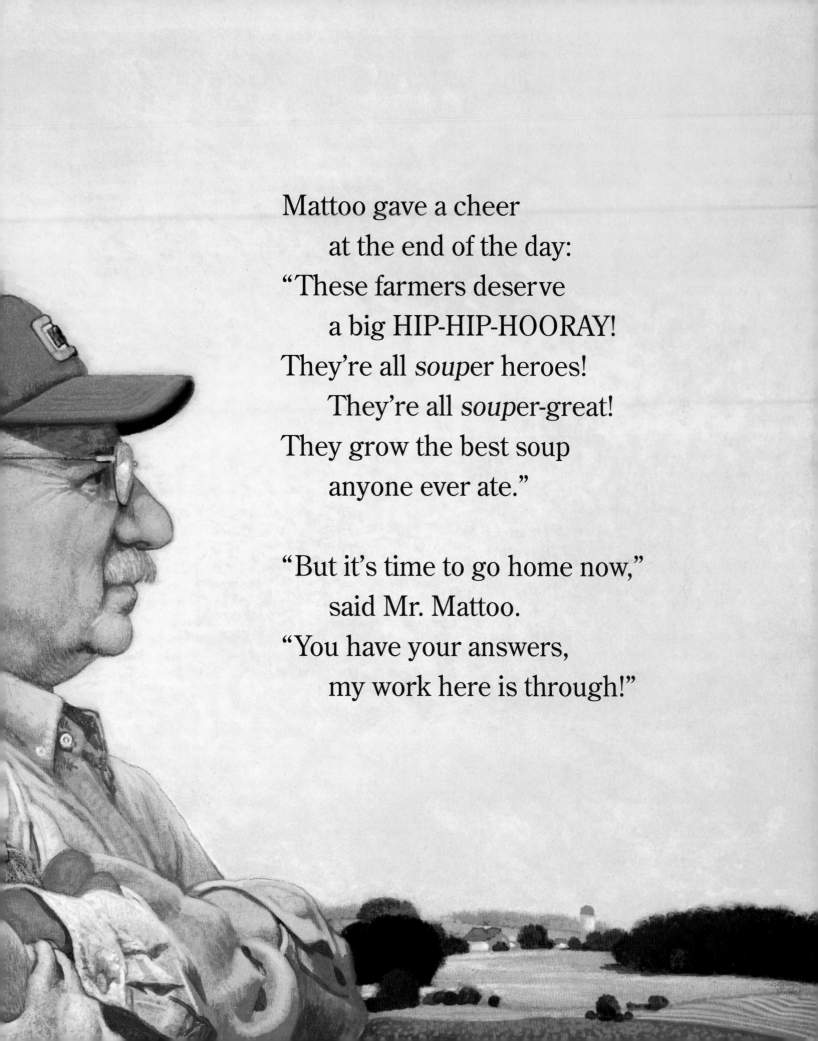

Mattoo gave a cheer
    at the end of the day:
"These farmers deserve
    a big HIP-HIP-HOORAY!
They're all *souper* heroes!
    They're all *souper*-great!
They grow the best soup
    anyone ever ate."

"But it's time to go home now,"
    said Mr. Mattoo.
"You have your answers,
    my work here is through!"

And then, just like that, Phin was back in his chair
and that big bowl of soup, steaming hot, was still there.
"Guess I'll have to try it," said Phineas Quinn.
So he opened his mouth and he spooned some soup in.

He swallowed,
   he sighed…
      he knew he'd been beaten.
That soup was the best thing that he'd ever eaten!
   Phin said, "Hey, how come we've never had this before?"
His mom, she just laughed, then she served him some more.

So if you are someone who thinks soup is scary,
  if facing a bowl makes you worried and wary —
Take some soup in your spoon,
  put the spoon to your lips,
and then say these words, right out loud,
  between sips:

"Who grew my soup?
  That's what I'd like to know.
Who grew my soup?
  That's where I'd like to go!"

And a souped-up balloon might drop down from the blue,
   with a friendly old fellow named Mr. Mattoo
who will take you aboard, and then zoom off with you.

        It might…
            It might not…
        But still, either way,
            any day you eat soup
                is a *soup*er good day!

Grant Hitchner and his family have been growing carrots and other vegetables for Campbell's soup for three generations. He has also raised an impressive crop of daughters — six of them! Daughter Kristen works the farm daily with her father. Her sisters often help out at harvest time.

Phillip Perez has been growing tomatoes for Campbell's soup for more than 40 years. He and his son John farm 1,700 acres, and each acre can produce nearly 80,000 pounds of tomatoes! Phillip's favorite soup is — you guessed it — tomato.

If you rearrange the letters of the name **Mattoo**, you'll find they spell the name of the first soup Campbell's ever made, more than 100 years ago.

Tom Darbyshire was born and raised in the small farming town of Moultrie, Georgia. Although both his father and grandfather were livestock veterinarians and farmers, Tom somehow ended up working in New York City as Senior Creative Director at BBDO, where he creates advertising for Campbell's and other famous brand names. He loves his wife, two daughters, two dogs, and soup.

C. F. Payne, award-winning artist, caricaturist, and illustrator, adds his unique touch to this tasty tale. Mr. Payne's work has appeared in *Time, Rolling Stone, Sports Illustrated*, and *National Geographic* magazines. His portraits can be found in galleries throughout the USA, most notably the Norman Rockwell Museum and the National Portrait Gallery. In addition to his renowned portraits, C. F. Payne has illustrated numerous children's books, including *The Remarkable Farkle McBride* and *Micawber* written by John Lithgow. He currently resides in Cincinnati, Ohio, with his wife, Paula, and children.